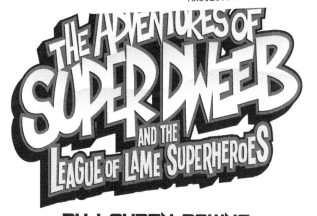

BY LAUREN DOWNS
ILLUSTRATIONS/COVER BY TIM READ

For all the Super Dweebs of the world -
Stay Super!

-LD

CONTENTS

CHAPTER 1:
THE ADVENTURE BEGINS

The kid is an outcast, a nerd, a nobody. Suddenly he gets some incredible superpowers, and BAM! The outcast is now the hero. He gets the girl, friends start lining up, he aces all his classes, and everything works out like a fairytale.

Sound familiar? I've seen that story more times than I can count in books, comics, and movies—pretty much in all kinds of media from the olden days… but my life happens to be the complete opposite.

I'm Dwayne. Dwayne Richardson. I'm 11 years old and it's the year 3219. I live in a place called the Aethur, which just happens to be a world full of superheroes. Pretty awesome, right? Everyone I know has some kind of superpower—my parents, my friends, I think even my baby sister could have them. It seems like the whole world has superpowers… except for me. Kids can start developing powers even when they're babies. Most kids have them at full capacity at least by the 3rd grade. But me? I'm in the 6th grade this year, and when it comes to powers, I've got zip, zero, zilch. My parents say I'm just a "late bloomer," that my powers just haven't shown up yet, but I'm starting to think that I might just be… a normal kid.

Let me explain how my world came to exist. You see, back in the year 2626, this planet called Earth had billions of humans living on it and they didn't take the best care of it. The planet was suffering. Eventually, the oceans and rivers on the planet were filling with garbage, much of the wildlife had gone extinct, and a lot of the people were starving. Something drastic had to happen. So, a big company called the Aethura Project decided that humans had outgrown the Earth and needed to find to an entirely different planet that was bigger and could handle more people. Sending out thousands of spaceships, they left the Earth on a mission to explore new planets which might have the necessary elements like oxygen and water for people to survive. It took many years and many failed attempts, but finally, in the year 2765 they discovered a whole new solar system with a planet a lot like the Earth. This planet had water, trees, oxygen, and gravity. It also happened to be nearly three times the size of Earth, so it could support many more people. The Aethura Project called the planet the Aethur. Taking as many humans as they could fit on spaceships, they flew away to begin anew, leaving the Earth and its few remaining inhabitants abandoned.

As the years passed, and the people who colonized the Aethur began settling down and having families, they noticed something strange was happening. Many of the children born on the planet began developing odd abilities. What people didn't realize about the Aethur was that the planet's core is made of Plutonium, which is radioactive.

This long-term radioactive exposure caused numerous mutations in the children, which over time manifested into all sorts of unique abilities. Eventually, as the generations passed, every person on the planet had developed some type of superpower, and that is how the Aethurians came to be a race of superhumans.

CHAPTER 2:
A FAMILY OF SUPERHEROES

People with super powers tend to fall into two categories. On one side you've got your heroes. On the other side, the villains. I've noticed that you can usually tell what kind of person someone is going to be by the powers they develop. I mean, take the superhero-types, for example. They typically get really cool stuff like a strong sense of justice, flight, and super strength. While the supervillain's powers might be pretty cool too, like being able to freeze people or set things on fire with your eyeballs, their powers are definitely creepier. Finally, there are other people who fall into those two categories, but because they have less impressive powers, tend to end up as a sidekick for a superhero, or as a villain's minion.

Now, you would think that with two very different types of people in the world, with two very opposing missions in life, that people would always stick with their own kind. Superheroes with superheroes and villains with villains, and honestly, that's typically true. But not in my family. My parents say that our family is a severe case of when opposites attract. You see, my dad's a superhero, while my mom's a supervillain. My dad works as a judge in our courts determining who's right or wrong in really tough cases. It's perfect for him since his superpower is a super strong sense of justice. My mom, however, is entirely different. She works in a secret lab making cool viruses and weapons to sell to the highest bidder. I don't really know all the specifics, because it's, well, secret. My dad says it's immoral, but Mom's reply is always that it's just business.

You might wonder how people so opposite from each other could stay together—it's like a Republican and a Democrat living in harmony; It seems impossible. But, by focusing on what they love about each other and forgiving the rest, they make it work. Dad said he fell in love with Mom from the first moment he set eyes on her. She had her new prototype of the disintegration laser she had just created pointed at his head. When he looked up at her and "gazed upon her beautiful face" (*insert finger in mouth and make gagging noise here*), he said he just stood there smiling like an idiot. It surprised her so much that she didn't even complain when he came to his senses, slowly took the prototype away, crushed it, and threw it in the trash can. Then, they went for coffee and have been a team ever since.

I'm not really a hero or a villain, not even a sidekick. Honestly, I'm not even qualified to be somebody's pet. I'm just Dwayne. Dwayne the Ordinary. I'm not particularly good at anything either. I'm not smart (though Mom says I just need to "apply myself"), not good-looking, not tall, not short. I'm just… below average in every way by today's standards.

I'm the only one in my grade who hasn't "bloomed" yet. Maybe it's a puberty thing? Or maybe I'm always going to be like this. Either way, I usually just try not to think about it. The way I see it, if it's meant to be, it'll happen, and if not, I'll just have to live with it. I try to be positive and all, but that doesn't mean I don't still daydream about having superpowers. I mean, I do have a special notebook full of doodles of "Super Dwayne" doing tons of heroic things, which is pretty much my ultimate wish. A superhero me with all of the best powers there could ever be.
Hey, a guy can dream.

CHAPTER 3:
THE LEAGUE OF
LAME SUPERHEROES

Honestly, my life isn't all that bad. I do have a couple of really good friends. Todd Perry has been my best friend since we had desks next to each other in kindergarten. He's a short, chubby kid with red curly hair and a face full of freckles. The girls all say, "he's so cute,"

but unfortunately, I think it's more of a "cute puppy" cute than a "I want to go out with you" type of cute. But that hasn't stopped him from giving all the girls in our class flowers or chocolate in an attempt to "woo" them. Sadly, his quest for a girlfriend will probably remain unsuccessful simply because of his superpower.

His big superpower is that he can sense when danger's coming, which is pretty cool... However, how he senses danger is not. Whenever danger approaches, his feet will start to stink. At the first hint of danger, it's not so bad, but the worse the danger gets, the worse his feet stink. And let me tell you, I've been with him in some pretty dangerous situations and I'm honestly not sure that facing that danger would have been easier than smelling his feet. Take rotten eggs, spoiled milk, and one of my sister's dirty diapers, then multiply that stink by ten! It can get NASTY! All of the guys in class call him Toejam. I'm sure you can imagine why. Toejam's power isn't completely useless though, He has sensed a pop quiz coming in class before, which has saved me and our other friend, Hero, on more than one occasion.

Hero's a really tall guy, with long, straight black hair, and he's as skinny as a pole. His full name is Hiromasa Long, which is quite a mouthful and you might think we call him Hero for short. But that's not how he got his name. You see, Hero's a pretty compassionate guy and when we were all in the 2nd grade, there was this huge spider on the windowsill in one of our classes. A couple of people were freaking out, refusing to sit anywhere near it. This started to make all the girls panic. So, Hero bravely walked over to the spider, gently picked it up with a napkin and set it free outside. When he came

10

back, the guys hi-fived him and the girls started calling him "their hero." Of course, the rest of us couldn't let that slide, and all of the guys in class made a pact to tease him relentlessly. We called him "our Hero" every chance we could. Over time we dropped the "our" and he's just been Hero ever since.

Hero's big superpower is that he can talk to undersea creatures. And I guess it's a pretty cool power if you think about it, but we don't live anywhere near the oceans or any large bodies of water. There are a few lakes and ponds, but nothing cool. So, other than talking to his pet goldfish, Hero's power is pretty much as useless as Toejam's. But hey, at least they have a power… I can't even boast that.

The three of us are pretty much our own club. We call ourselves the League of Lame Superheroes and we do everything together. We're like the three amigos, with a bond that can never be broken! Although this all sounds pretty care-free, the League of Lame Superheroes does not exist in a perfect, crime-free utopia. No, every day the League of Lame Superheroes must navigate the most dangerous, aggressive, treacherous place on the planet… middle school.

CHAPTER 4:
SCHOOL SUCKS

Every day, The League of Lame Superheroes must band together, battle darkness, and defend ourselves from our evil nemeses… the school bullies!

Let me begin with Chris. He's a really tall, really buff football star, with shaggy brown hair and dark eyes that make all the girls swoon. His power is, of course, superhuman strength. Once, he lifted a bleacher with one hand! Not impressed? Well our entire class was sitting on it, including our teacher, Mrs. Sharp, who has to weigh at least 6000lbs! He just stood there posing for pictures and never even broke a sweat. We call him "the Brawn," though his real name is Christian Mercia. You would think that with that name and that super power that he'd be some really nice guy, right? Maybe like a gentle giant? Wrong. Chris is the most un-merciful guy I know! He once held Toejam upside down by his ankles for fifteen minutes. He didn't let him go until Toejam's feet started stinking so bad that they were making Chris' eyes water! Chris ended up tossing Toe in a dumpster, claiming that he'd smell better after rolling around in the trash for a while. Which was true, but still really mean.

Chris is awful, but he's not the only villain the League of Lame Superheroes has to combat every day. There's also Melvin Pearce, a very small, very short kid with massively thick glasses, huge buck teeth and blond hair that he keeps in a buzz cut. He's a total nerd. His superpower is that he's insanely good at math. When teachers used to hand out multiplication and division worksheets, those ones where you have a minute to

complete as many questions as you can, Melvin would
have all 50 finished before most of us could get through
the first three and it only took him that long because he
couldn't write that fast. Now, for a middle school guy, that
would be a useful power.

   We call him "the Brain." Because of the math thing
and he's the brains behind the bullying operation. Chris
is just the muscle and gladly does Melvin's bidding. He
and Chris have been friends (or should I say, "partners
in crime") since the 4th grade. Rumor has it that the

only reason they're friends at all is that Melvin does all of Chris' homework and in exchange, Chris muscles kids out of their lunch money so Melvin can pocket it himself. Whatever the reason they're friends, together they make our lives miserable.

Hero, Toejam, and I have asked our teachers for help with "the Brains and Brawn" countless times; however, their solution is just to send us to Principal Mason. Unfortunately, every time we speak to him, it's like hitting a rock wall...literally! His superpower is that his whole body is made of stone. He's extremely tough, and rumor has it that he's been around for millions of years, but no one knows for certain. Sadly, he thinks kids these days are too soft and need to toughen up, so he doesn't really take a stance against bullying.

I'm pretty sure that everyone in class would love to see justice served to Melvin and Chris, but it looks like Principal Mason won't be any help. Until we find some other way to expel our bullies, we'll just have to use our dealings with them to practice fighting evil. Hey, every superhero has to start somewhere, right?

The kids in my class have a variety of superpowers. Laura Windsor's ability is persuasion. She can convince anyone of anything. Once, she convinced Mr. Tate, the biology teacher, that he was in love with his trash can He spent the entire day walking around hugging and kissing it. There's also Thatcher Holt, whose power is sharpshooting (he never misses); Blake Graham, who has precognition (he can see what happens before it happens); and Lucy Gonzales, who has explosive farts. That one's a pretty hilarious power. Silent but deadly? No, ALL of them are deadly! Pretty hard to be discrete when you've got to try not to blow up the school. She almost joined the League of Lame Superheroes, but in the end decided that we were even too lame for her.

Anyway, now that you know my situation, I'm sure you can see why school is such a challenge for me. I'm at the bottom of the food chain socially and getting decent grades seems nearly impossible. The teachers never grade on a curve. I mean, there's really no point because some kid like Caitlin Bird, who has a photographic memory, is just going to break it anyway.

I actually have a huge test next week in history, and I'm pretty sure I'm going to bomb it. It's hard enough to pay attention in class during a subject as boring as history. But toss in my teacher Mr. Hammond, and it's near impossible! His superpower is supposed to be that he can control the weather (which is why we've never had a snow day on test day), but I'm convinced that his real superpower is the ability to put anyone to sleep with his monotone voice. He just drones on and on… I can never keep up. I always end up doodling in a notebook instead of paying attention, but I can't help it. It's way easier to doodle than it is to do history.

Though I like to doodle, I'm not much of an artist, but I can make a pretty decent stick man. Other than that, I pretty much suck at everything. I'm not good at writing… or math, or history, or geography, or… well, okay, you get the point. I'm not really good at anything. My mom keeps encouraging me to "find my passion," but whatever it is, I don't think I can find it at school.

Anyway, now you know me. Dwayne the Ordinary.

CHAPTER 5:

A DAY IN THE LIFE OF ME

BEEP... BEEP... BEEP...

Ugh. Waking up for school is the worst. One minute, you're in dreamland, soaring over the city, the ground far below you, the rush of wind in your face... and then, the screeching alarm blares, jolting you back to cold, cruel reality.

Waking up in my tiny bedroom, I sighed, wanting nothing in life as much as just going back to sleep. Instead, I rolled over and hit the alarm clock, sitting up on the edge of my sleep pod.

Padding over to my closet, I pulled out my clothes for the day. Jeans. A blue-and-white-striped t-shirt. Socks with retro spaceships on them and my favorite tennis shoes. Perfect. As I grabbed my backpack, I headed from the safety of my room and closed the door behind me.

Mom was in the kitchen making breakfast. "Good morning, honey," she sang as she placed a stack of waffles in front of me.

"Where's dad?" I hummed, dousing the waffles with imitation maple syrup.

"Oh, you know him," she said, rolling her eyes.

"Off saving the world, I'm sure." Then added with a touch of annoyance, "He was supposed to drop your sister at daycare today, but he flew out of here spouting his typical morning catchphrase about how 'Justice can't wait.'" I just nodded and finished my breakfast. Suddenly, a honk outside startled me, I didn't realize it was so late.

"Oh, that's the bus- hurry up, honey, you don't

want to miss it!" Mom called, ushering me towards the front door and sticking my notebook in my hand.

"And don't forget about the parent-teacher conference!" she yelled as I ran for the hoverbus, which was hovering a foot off the ground right in front of my house, waiting for me to board.

Hopping on, I went straight to the third row where I knew I would find Toejam and Hero waiting for me.

"Hey guys," I panted, out of breath, and plopped down between them.

"Hey D," Toe smiled back.

"You ready for the parent-teacher conference tonight?" Hero grimaced. "You nervous?"

"Nah, come on, everybody's doing bad this year. They can't single me out just because I'm the powerless wonder," I laughed nervously. "Besides, I've got a C- or a D in almost every class. That's not THAT bad, right?"

"Aren't you failing history?" Toe asked, raising one brow.

"Well, yeah, but I mean, how can ANYBODY pay attention when Mr. H is going on and on about World War III?"

"I just try to stare at his unibrow. It wiggles around like an enormous worm on his face when he talks, and by staring at it, it at least looks like I'm paying attention," Toe laughed.

"His eyebrows are probably the only lively thing about him," I muttered back. "I mean, he's got to be, like, a hundred years old."

"Two hundred," Hero shook his head.

As the hoverbus sailed over the rooftops towards the school building, stopping occasionally to pick up

17

students along the way, we made plans to have a sleepover that night where we could play our favorite video game. Before long, we had arrived. Standing to exit the bus, we stepped onto the pavement and headed inside.

I had just entered the building when I felt an all-too-familiar smack on the back of my head, causing me to drop my notebook. Turning around, I was just in time to see Melvin snatch my notebook from the floor and start flipping through it.

"Well if it isn't 'Brains and Brawn,'" I muttered, rubbing the back of my head, sure I would have a bruise.

"Hey!" Toejam protested, attempting to grab my notebook back, but Chris easily plucked it from his hands and proceeded to hold it menacingly above his head.

"Give it back," Hero spoke coldly, extending a hand for it.

"Oh, not so fast," Chris grinned, as he flipped through the pages. "What the heck is this?" He jeered as he held up a doodle I'd created of a stickman wearing a cape and flying over the city. I had scribbled "Super Dwayne" all over the picture in different fonts.

People were gawking. Everyone who'd just come off of the bus was watching, laughing and pointing at the humiliating drawing.

My cheeks burned with red-hot embarrassment. In anger, I clenched my fists. It was hard not to explode then and there, but somehow, I kept my cool. Somehow.

"Are you kidding? Super Dwayne?" Melvin cackled. "Believe me, you are anything but super. You'll probably never even get powers. Or if you do, I am sure they will be equally as useless as you are."

Chris ripped the page from the notebook, wadded

it into a ball, and pitched it into the nearest trash can. "Super Dwayne?" He cackled as he tossed the notebook to the floor. "More like Super Dweeb."

I crouched to pick up my notebook, grimacing at the missing page.

"Hey, don't worry about them," Hero said softly. "They don't know what they're talking about."

"Yeah, they're just being JERKS," Toe spat at the duo. "They're just bullies, you know? Come on... Let's get to class."

Then, I remembered something my dad told me about bullies. "You know, Dwayne," he'd said, "most of the time, people just want to see a reaction out of you. If you don't respond the way they expect, a lot of times, they'll just get bored and leave you alone." Well, this seemed like a good time to try his advice.

      I looked up and started chuckling, then I started laughing. Hard. Like, bent in two with tears running down my face, laughing. "Super Dweeb! That's hilarious!" I chortled. "Oh my gosh, that's actually perfect, you know? Cause I'm like, not really good at anything. You guys don't mind if I use that, do you?" By this time, Hero and Toejam were rolling along with me, while the "Brains and Brawn" just stood there, dumbfounded.

      Then the most amazing thing happened. Chris just mumbled, "Whatever, idiot," turned around, and walked away with Melvin right on his heels. It was awesome! Throwing our arms over each other's shoulders, my friends and I headed off to class, laughing all the way.

CHAPTER 6:
YOU SAY YOU WANNA ESSAY?

Entering English class and plopping down in our seats, we began our daily ritual of cracking jokes at our teacher's expense. Each day, we placed bets on what gaudy jewelry she would be wearing. Would it be the nasty "vintage" pendant with an actual green beetle sealed inside, or would it be the chunky gold necklace that she claimed was real, even though it always turned her wrinkly neck green? Gross! And the winner was... Hero (he guessed the pendant).

"Good morning, class. Today, we are going to be writing essays," Mrs. Walker warbled, squinting at us from behind her ultra-thick glasses. She was as blind as a bat; however, she did have super human hearing, which was a pain because she always knew if someone was whispering or playing on their communicator instead of doing their schoolwork. But she didn't need her super hearing to hear the collective groans caused by her announcement. Ignoring our protests, she continued.

"There are five parts to a basic essay," she began. After what seemed like 10,000 hours, she finally stopped talking long enough to notice the glazed looks in our eyes and the puddle of drool leaking off the top of Toejam's desk, where he face-planted 20 minutes before. Thankfully, she passed out a handout to help us out and let us get to work on our own.

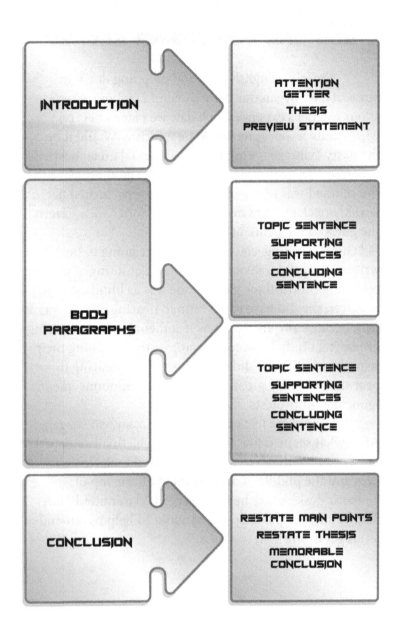

INTRODUCTION

ATTENTION GETTER
THESIS
PREVIEW STATEMENT

BODY PARAGRAPHS

TOPIC SENTENCE
SUPPORTING SENTENCES
CONCLUDING SENTENCE

TOPIC SENTENCE
SUPPORTING SENTENCES
CONCLUDING SENTENCE

CONCLUSION

RESTATE MAIN POINTS
RESTATE THESIS
MEMORABLE CONCLUSION

Okay... This is easy enough. It's just an essay. Everybody writes essays... right?

"Remember, an essay can have as many body points as you like, as long as it contains at least two. Most often, a basic essay will have three main points. However, for this assignment, your essays will only have two main points: one paragraph about a problem you faced, and a second paragraph about how you handled it. Your essay will still need an introduction and a conclusion as well. Your essays will be due Monday. Good luck!" And with this, she dismissed the moaning, grumbling class with an entire essay to write over the weekend. Great.

"So, what are you guys going to write about?" Hero asked. "I'm going to write about that time my brother's ferret got into my backpack and I didn't know it. I was sitting in Mr. Melton's science class when Chelsea McGuffin started screaming and pointing and jumped up on her desk. Then I saw what she was freaking out about. The ferret had snuck out of my backpack and was running through the class. It took six people to corner and catch it. Then, I had to spend the rest of the day carrying the dumb thing around in my hoodie pocket. It was so embarrassing. It also ate my math homework! At least I had the ferret for proof, but it took me an hour to redo it when I got home, and Mrs. Webster still took off 10% because it was 'technically' late."

"I'm going to write about the one and only time I agreed to babysit my little sister." Toe chimed in. "She wanted chocolate milk, and while I was making it, she got into the trash, then while I was cleaning that up, she got into the chocolate syrup and smeared it all over herself and the living room, so then I had to go and clean that up, and then give her a bath. And her diaper! I swear, my dad took her to CrystaI Hut and fed her a bunch of sliders for lunch. It was utterly the evilest, most disgusting, repulsive thing on the planet. And the smell… Aghh, I still have nightmares! What about you, Dwayne?"

"I have no idea," I answered honestly.

"Well, you don't have a lot of time, but you'll figure it out," Hero shrugged.

Stepping into the cafeteria, we slipped into line to get our meals. For lunch today, the cafeteria was serving pizza. Okay, it wasn't real pizza, but nutrition blocks, which is a big block of nutrients that gets infused with some sort of flavor to make them taste less disgusting. It doesn't work. They're nasty. The flavors today were different varieties of pizza. I got pepperoni, of course, Hero chose sausage, and Toejam went for cheese, probably because it smelled like his feet.

"I hear we get out after next class today," Toe grinned. "I mean, we still have to sit through Mr. Hammond's boring history lecture, but at least we get out early for the parent-teacher conference."

"Yeah, it's better than a full day of class, I guess, but I really am nervous about the conference," I grimaced as I took a bite of my nutrient block, not sure if the grimace was because of the conference or my lunch. It tasted like pizza-flavored dirt.

"Hey, Super Dweeb," Chris approached, towering over the three of us with Melvin lurking at his side like a little pet rat. "Give me your lunch money."

"You're too late, Chris," I replied smoothly with a shrug. "Already spent it. Try again next week."

"Excuse me?" he laughed. "I don't think you heard

me right. Lunch money. Five bucks, cough it up. Or I'm going to stick your head in a toilet."

Threatening a swirly at lunch time? He was bluffing and I was feeling brave after this morning. "You wouldn't dare," I volleyed back. "There are teachers right over there, you know," I said, nodding in the direction of the teachers. "Get lost."

Chris cast a glance towards the teachers' table, where the professors were eating and talking quietly among themselves. Then, narrowing his eyes at me, he relented. "Fine," he smirked, "But you're definitely going to pay." Evidently it wasn't worth making a scene in front of the teachers, so he stomped away, Melvin obediently following behind like a puppy.

Toe clapped me on the back, Hero grinned, and I tried to calm my heart, which was about to beat out of my chest. "Nice one!" Toe cheered.

I guess it was a small victory for the little guys.

History class was a snooze. I nearly fell asleep in the back of the classroom, daydreaming about Super Dwayne flying across the sky above the buildings far below.

Mr. H droned on and on in his boring, monotonous voice about World War III resulting in nuclear warfare between all of the world powers, which caused mass extinctions of many species, including the… blah blah blah … and this led to World War IV, where another nuclear war caused intense radiation that… blah blah blah.

We get it. The wars caused radiation that killed a bunch of animal species and polluted everything and prompted the humans to move to the Aethur. Why do professors have to be so long-winded? Couldn't everything important just be summed up in one sentence? I mean, why do we need to know all of the little events that led up to everything? Who cares who did this, who said that and what little fights escalated to a war? It's all over now anyway, does it even matter anymore?

Finally, the bell rang and we all rushed out of the classroom, ready for the weekend. But first, I had to survive the dreaded parent-teacher conference. As we headed to the lobby to meet up with our parents, the League of Lame Superheroes plotted our weekend adventures.

"You guys still coming over to my place tonight?" Hero asked, to which Toe and I enthusiastically nodded.

"Wouldn't miss it," I grinned. "You can hear about my mom chewing me out after the conference because of my terrible grades."

"Mine too, probably," Toe frowned. "I hope not too much though. I don't like getting in trouble…"

"Come on, Toe, when are you ever in trouble?" I laughed. Then, spotting my mom, I waved goodbye to Hero and Toe and I reluctantly departed to face my doom.

A few minutes later, I was slumped in a chair, facing the firing squad, with my life on the line. As the school counselor and principal sat menacingly across the table, I was sure that sheer joy was evident on their faces as they sat smiling, relishing in the discomfort of my torment. Mr. Simpson, the counselor, was a short, bald, pudgy guy that always looked like he was angry.

"Mrs. Richardson," he began in a slow drawl, his snakelike gaze drifting over to me, like a predator analyzing his prey. "Your son isn't doing well in school, not well at all. He has C's in most of his classes, many of them C minuses. A D in Math. And… he's failing History."

I wasn't too surprised to hear that. Math wasn't my best subject. And History was just… boring. I don't see why we need to know every little event since the dawn of time… and it's just going to keep getting harder as time passes. That's the "beauty" of history, I guess. But I think it's terrible.

"Unless he can pull his grade up by the end of the semester, I am afraid that he will be forced to repeat the sixth grade." He announced with barely subdued pleasure.

"Wait, what? Repeat sixth grade?" I wailed with absolute panic. Okay Mr. Simpson, that one hit hard. Real hard. It felt like his words had physically punched me, knocking the wind out of me, and leaving me hyperventilating. Repeat the sixth grade?! How the heck was I supposed to do that?! I'd be behind everyone else, I'd be a laughing stock, and worst of all, Toe and Hero would move on without me. I'd probably just end up failing History again and then I'd have to repeat it all over again. It would be like being stuck in a permanent loop, doomed, living a nightmare forever!

"Is there anything that we can do about this?" my mother inquired with intense concern. "What is the next step?"

"His history final is on Monday," the principal said, shaking his head. "If he can manage an A on his exam, I think it will pull his grade up enough to pass."

An A? I've never gotten an A on a history test in my life! This is impossible!

"Certainly. I will speak to my husband and be sure

he spends the entire weekend studying," my mom agreed, nodding her head. Then, just like a revolving door, we were escorted from the room and the next family was ushered in to hear about all of the things their kid was doing wrong.

This was by far the worst day of my life.

CHAPTER 7:
PLANS FOR THIS PREDICAMENT

My mom just drove along, in a daze, shaking her head as we headed home in her hovercar. "Dwayne, I know you struggle in school, but failing is unacceptable. Have you spoken to your teacher about your grades?"

"Well, no, but... Mom, you don't understand! I don't even have powers, it's not my fault! The other kids always break the curve!"

"Don't make excuses, Dwayne. We will be talking to your father about this. I don't think it's a good idea for you to stay the night at Hero's tonight. You need to be studying instead."

"Mom! Please let me go, we've been planning this for weeks…" I felt like my life was falling apart around me. I might have to repeat the 6th grade, I wasn't going to get to hang out with Hero and Toe, and then they were going to go onto 7th grade without me and leave me all by myself. And I still had a stupid essay to write this weekend. Wait. That's it! The essay!

"Mom, please can I go? I have an essay to write for English and Hero, Toe, and I were going to do them together."

She paused, seeming to think about it. But in the end, I knew she couldn't say no to it if schoolwork were involved, and it worked. She finally nodded her consent. "Alright, Dwayne, but I'm picking you up first thing in the morning, and you're going to spend all day studying for your History final. And I'll expect to see that essay tomorrow morning as well."

Well, that just backfired, but at least I could

hang out with the guys. "Okay, I'll show it to you in the morning." I mumbled. I guessed even if we had to waste some of our video game-playing time to write stupid essays, at least we'd be together. This sleepover had just become really important. I mean, if Hero and Toe went on to 7th grade without me, it could be our last.

CHAPTER 8:
SLEEPOVER STUDY SESSION

"Bye mom," I waved as I stepped in the door, breathing a sigh of relief once it closed behind me. The sleepover was happening, and I hadn't been forced to stay home.

"C'mon Dwayne," Hero called from his living room, already sitting on the couch with Toejam beside him. "You guys ready to play Star Cadets XXVII? It's finally out."

"Yeah! We've got all night to beat it!" Toe cheered, "Come on! I call player 2."

"I can't," I sighed, flopping down on the couch beside Toe. "Guys, I've got bad news... I'm failing history."

"Yeah, no duh," Hero snickered. "You fall asleep in class half the time."

"And the other half, you stare out the window," Toejam chimed in. "Do you pay attention in there at all?"

"Whatever, that isn't important. But apparently, I have to ace the history final or else... I'm going to have to repeat the 6th grade."

"WHAT?!" My wide eyed friends yelled in unison.

"Oh man- How did this happen?!" Hero choked, clearly upset.

"You mean we might have to go on without you?" Toe was so panicked that he looked like he might cry. "But you're my best friend!" he moaned and then catching himself, quickly added, "Uh, no offense, Hero."

"Ummm, none taken," Hero responded sarcastically with a dramatic eye roll. "So, what are you going to do, man?"

"Well," I began. "My mom says I have to write the essay tonight. She almost didn't let me come. But I begged her. She's coming to get me early in the morning, and she said I have to show her the essay first thing. And to make things worse, I have to study history all weekend until my brain turns to mush." I complained, then quickly added, "But I REALLY don't want to repeat the 6th grade, so I'll do anything!"

"Well, maybe we can all write our essays together," Hero suggested.

"Yeah, and then maybe we'll have time to play our game and stuff," Toe added.

"Thanks guys," I grinned. "The League of Lame Superheroes has to conquer its greatest battle yet... the English essay."

"Okay, so, the first thing we've got to do is think about topics to write about. Some kind of challenge we faced and how we handled it," Hero hummed. "I still think I'm going to write about my brother's ferret."

"Uh, challenges... Yeah, I'm probably still going to write about my little sister. That's the most challenging thing I've ever done," Toejam decided aloud. "What about you, any bright ideas, Dwayne?"

I thought about it... but my mind went blank.

"Ugh! I don't have a clue!" I whined.

"Alright, well what's the first thing you're supposed to do when you want to come up with ideas?" Toe asked. Hero and I just stood there, blank-faced, staring at him. "Mrs. Walker was talking about it last week in English," Toejam prodded.

Oh yeah, what was that? It had something to do with the weather. Brain raining. No, that's not right. Brain clouding. No, that's not it either. Oh, Brainstorming! Yes, that's it!

"Brainstorming!" I yelled, thrilled that I remembered.

"Yeah, you got it!" Toe cheered, hi-fiving me.

"How do you brainstorm again?" Hero asked.

"You get out paper and write down everything that comes to your mind whether you think it's good or lame. You just write down as many ideas as you can possibly come up with." Toe explained.

So, that's what we did. I got a sheet of paper and started writing down every little problem I could think of. Our arch nemeses, the school bullies, also known as the Brains and the Brawn. My cat getting stuck up a tree. Running out of milk after I already poured a bowl of cereal. Having to write this stupid essay. Failing history and having to repeat the sixth grade! "I guess I could write about my history final, but I don't know the outcome yet. Or something to do with Brains and Brawn."

"You could write about this morning when we got off the hoverbus. You handled that pretty well," Hero suggested. "They couldn't get the best of you."

"That's a good idea," I agreed. "Okay, I'll do that." Now, HOW do I do that?

I pulled out my English handout outlining the parts of a basic essay.

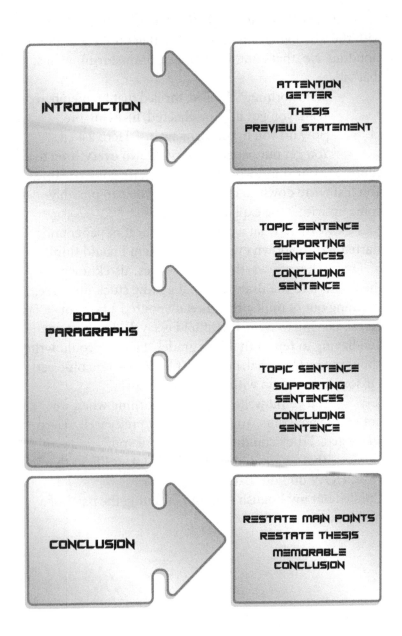

INTRODUCTION

ATTENTION GETTER
THESIS
PREVIEW STATEMENT

BODY PARAGRAPHS

TOPIC SENTENCE
SUPPORTING SENTENCES
CONCLUDING SENTENCE

TOPIC SENTENCE
SUPPORTING SENTENCES
CONCLUDING SENTENCE

CONCLUSION

RESTATE MAIN POINTS
RESTATE THESIS
MEMORABLE CONCLUSION

I figured we would start by writing the introduction, because that's where you introduce your thesis statement. Mrs. Walker said the thesis is the most important part of the essay because it's the overall idea of the entire paper. A sentence explaining what your essay is about. Also, you have to restate your thesis in the conclusion, but before you can restate it, you have to figure out what your thesis is. Since the thesis is the biggest part of the introduction, I figured we would start there.

"First is the introduction. We need to do an attention-getter, a thesis, and a preview statement," I noted. "Do you guys remember what these things are?"

"Well, attention-getter is pretty self-explanatory, guys. You need to put something in there that's going to get people's attention and make them want to read the rest of your essay. Mrs. Walker said it's also called a hook and that it's a really crucial part of a good essay." Toe replied. I am so glad he actually pays attention in English class. "Start with your thesis."

So, I started thinking about what I thought the main point of my essay was and I decided that it was what my dad said about the way to handle bullies. Cool, I had a thesis. "I've got a thesis!" I shouted triumphantly, "I'm ready to write my introduction."

"Uhh, okay," Toejam murmured as he began looking over the handout. "I heard it's best to start with an outline, BEFORE you start to write." Why was he looking at me like I was a complete dork?

"So, I guess we start our outline with the introduction, then," I suggested, skimming my handout. "It says we need an attention-getter?"

"Actually, Let's outline the introduction last," Hero suggested, "because we don't know what else we're introducing yet. So, it will be easier to start with the body paragraphs of the essay first and then come back and finish the introduction and conclusion. Nothing says it has to be done in order, as long as you have your thesis."

"Good idea," I answered, and started to outline my paragraphs.

Introduction. To come after I write my body paragraphs

Paragraph 1. Bullied every day at school
    A. Brains and Brawn bullied me this morning
    B. Brawn hit me in the head, causing me to drop my books
    C. Brains found notebook, teased me relentlessly about doodles
        1. Called me Super Dweeb and everybody laughed

Paragraph 2. How I dealt with it
    A. Remembered what Dad said about bullies
        1. Don't give them reaction they want
    B. Started to laugh like a fool
        1. Asked if I could use the nickname
    C. Bullies gave up and went away

Conclusion. I've been bullied in all kinds of ways by Brains and Brawn. What dad said is true—it does help to combat a bully when you don't react the way they want you to.

"Hey, guys, I think I'm done with my outline," I boasted, holding my paper up.

"Me too," Toejam said, proudly displaying his outline as well.

"Me three. Now time to write the actual essay,"

Hero replied.

"Uggh." Was our mutual response.

Deciding to write the body paragraphs first, I began perusing my trusty English hand out. It stated that a paragraph should be at least 3-5 sentences (but it could be more).

Sentence 1: Topic sentence
Sentence 2-4: Supporting Details
Sentence 5: Concluding sentence

I can't believe I'm going to tell you this, but my teacher was right. Having my thoughts written on the outline actually did make writing the essay a whole lot easier. It didn't take me much time at all, and I had the body paragraphs finished in no time and was ready to move on to the introduction and conclusion.

For the introduction, I already had my thesis, but as I looked at my handout, it said the first sentence should be an attention-getter. Oh man, I had no idea how to say something interesting enough to get people to want to keep reading my essay. Luckily, I was confident that victory was within my grasp. The League of Lame Superheroes would come to the rescue!

"Uh, guys?" I looked up from my page and my friends stopped their frantic scribbling.

"You done?" Hero asked, seeming impressed.

"I wish," was my response. "I'm not sure how to do an attention-getter."

"Well there are several types of attention getters." Toe answered. "You can use a quote, a joke, an anecdote, a statistic, a question, even a short story. I'm doing a quote," He continued, and then read us his introduction.

TOEJAM'S INTRODUCTION

"Todd, your father and I need you to do us a small favor. It shouldn't be any trouble." That's how it all began, the epic babysitting misadventure which gives me nightmares to this day. I thought it would be easy, just keeping an eye on my sweet, innocent little sister for a few short hours, but boy was I wrong. When my parents got home, I was curled up in the fetal position, rocking back and forth, and mumbling about not being left alone with the little monster ever again. Let me tell you why.

"That's hilarious!" I laughed. I want to come up with something that good. "What about you Hero, do you have yours?"

"Yeah, I did a question."

HERO'S INTRODUCTION

What do you get when you combine a ferret, a backpack, and a science class? I had to find out the hard way, but at least I learned that even bad situations can have a silver lining. One day recently proved that old proverb was true.

"Oh, that one's good too," I worried aloud. "I'm gonna bomb this essay just with the first paragraph…"

"Hey man, that's not true," Toe replied, being encouraging, as always.

"Come on, you said you were writing about Brains and Brawn?" Hero tried to be practical. "How about a statistic on bullying or something? And then you can talk about your own experiences with them."

"Yeah, that's a good idea," I agreed, nodding my

head. I was glad that my friends were there to back me up. Making a quick search on my tablet, I found a good statistic on bullying, and my introduction went from there.

DWAYNE'S INTRODUCTION

Last year in 3218, 1 in 3 kids experienced some form of bullying in school. Despite centuries of attempts to remedy and destroy it, this one problem has plagued students since the dawn of mankind. My dad gave me some old advice about bullies that has still remained true: If you don't give them the reaction they're looking for, bullies will most often leave you alone. My dad's advice actually helped rescue me from a bullying experience a few days ago.

Now all that was left was the conclusion. The conclusion needed to review the main points of the essay, restate the thesis, and close with a thoughtful ending.

"Hey, Did you guys work on your conclusions yet?" I inquired.

"Yeah, here's mine," Toejam replied, reading his out loud.

TOEJAM'S CONCLUSION

Little superhumans can get into a load of trouble in a flash. You might think that babysitting is a pretty easy gig, but it's one of the most frightening nightmares of my life. Babysitting requires a level of bravery and skill that I do not possess, and in my opinion, is a job that is better left to the professionals.

"Okay, that was awesome," I howled.

"Wait, if you want funny, listen to mine," Hero chimed in.

HERO'S CONCLUSION

Despite the embarrassment, the eaten homework, and the fright of my life when that thing jumped out of my backpack, it wasn't a complete disaster. Turns out, girls think ferrets are pretty cute, and all the attention made Toejam super jealous, which was hilarious. In the end, good things really can come from bad situations. So, what DO you get when you combine a ferret, a backpack, and a science class? The answer—Four days of detention.

"Besides the part about me getting jealous, which so did not happen, that was a pretty good conclusion." Toe conceded.

"That was hilarious!" I howled, "And you sooooo did get jealous!"

Hearing the guys' conclusions helped, but now I had to finish my own conclusion. A few minutes later, I leapt up, holding my finished essay in the air with great enthusiasm, "I did it!" I exclaimed. "Are you guys done?"

"I've been done," Hero winked. "You guys are just slow."

"Not everybody's good at essays, Hero," Toe answered, still frantically scribbling on his paper.

"So, Mrs. Walker said you're always supposed to read your writing out loud when you're done so that you can hear any mistakes," Hero announced, recalling what our English teacher told us. "So, let's hear it, Dwayne."
A few moments of throat clearing later, I began to read.

"Last year in 3218, 1 in 3 kids experienced some form of bullying in school. Despite centuries of attempts to remedy and destroy it, this one problem has plagued students since the dawn of mankind. My dad gave me some advice about bullies that has always remained true: If you don't give them the reaction they're looking for, bullies will most often leave you alone. My dad's advice actually helped rescue me from a bullying experience a few days ago.

"I've been bullied at school every day since Kindergarten by the same two people, who my friends and I call "Brains and Brawn." Every day, they shove us around, demand our lunch money, and threaten us, and this day was no different. As soon as I walked in the doors, Brawn smacked the back of my head so hard that I dropped my books, scattering them all over the floor. Then, Brains snatched up my notebook, started looking through some doodles I had drawn, and noticed one where I'd written "Super Dwayne." Immediately, the bullies started to tease me and call me a "Super Dweeb" instead, which sucked because the hallways were full of people who were all staring at us, and some of them were laughing at me. I could feel my face getting hot, and I knew there was a decision I had to make on how to deal with this.

"I could get mad and upset, or I could do something they wouldn't expect. As I stood there humiliated, I remembered something my dad told me about dealing with bullies, and how you shouldn't give them the reaction they're trying to get out of you. So, I started to laugh really hard and asked them if I could use that nickname because it was so funny. Then I laughed even more, so much, in fact, that my friends couldn't help but join in. Pretty soon, the Brains and Brawn walked away, and people went back to doing whatever they were doing. I guess my dad was right. That was a good way of dealing with bullies because it worked.

"Despite all of the torturous ways I have suffered at the hands of Brains and Brawn, I have learned ways to deal with bullies. My dad's advice held true and I found the best way to handle a bully is to not give them the reaction they expect. Since the beginning of time, there have been bullies and though we can't completely eliminate the problem, we can reduce the way if affects us, just by how we react."

"Wow, dude! That was great!" Toe praised.

"Yeah, man, nice job! That's totally an 'A' paper!" Hero grinned.

"Sweet, thanks guys!" I beamed, proud of my essay.

After they read their papers and we made a few small fixes, I happily asked, "You guys ready to play Star Cadets XXVII?"

"Oh yeah, remember, I got dibs on player 2!" Toe called.

"Uggh, WE KNOW!!" Hero and I growled back.

Even though we had to spend a little time writing our essays, we still ended up having plenty of time to play our video games late into the evening until we eventually crashed on the couches. And, true to her word, my mom did arrive to get me very early the next morning. The good news was that I had the dreaded essay finished. The bad news was that a new torture was just beginning.

CHAPTER 9:
STUDY, STUDY, STUDY!

"Very nice work!" Mom smiled. "I'm proud of you for getting this done!"

I beamed up at her, relishing in this new, wonderful feeling I had as she praised my good work. And then, just as quickly as it began, it was squashed, demolished, utterly destroyed by her next words. "Now, I want you to sit down at the kitchen table and study, study, study!" she forcefully declared with a few strong thumps of her fingers on the table's linoleum top for emphasis. "I have to go to a business deal for work, but I'll be home in a few hours. Bye, sweetie." She gave me a kiss on the forehead before heading out the door. And thus, I was left to suffer all alone with just the echo of her fingers thumping the tabletop, her chant of "study, study, study!" in my ears.

I sighed as I sat at the kitchen table and stared at my boring history books. It seemed I was going to be in for a rough few hours, pouring over these boring facts. After just a few minutes, I found that as I turned the pages, the words seemed to run together, and I could hardly keep track of them all. Taking a deep breath, I decided to try something new. I was going to focus on finding just three facts from each chapter that I thought were important enough to write down and memorize. The first chapter was all about the Earth, the planet from where we all originated.

Chapter 1: The Earth is part of the Milky Way galaxy. The Earth is made up of 7 continents: North America, South America, Africa, Europe, Asia, Antarctica, and Australia. The Earth is made of about 70% water.

Okay, one chapter down. Not bad! It wasn't really so hard when I thought about it that way. Chapter 2 had information about earth's different continents. The third chapter discussed the Milky Way galaxy and all of the planets. Chapter 4 was all about NASA- the National Aeronautics and Space Administration, which was responsible for most of the world's early space exploration. Chapter 5 talked about humanity moving to the Aethur, where we live right now. And the rest of the chapters all talked about different parts of the Aethura project, all stuff we've already learned in school. In short, it was actually not as hard as I thought! I especially liked the chapter about NASA and space travel, so that part was much easier to read than the rest. How did I not hear about this in class? I guess I wasn't paying enough attention to realize we were actually talking about something cool.

After a few hours, I heard the door open, and my mom arrived home with my sister. I took a break from studying to play with her while mom made us lunch. Then my mom put my sister in her bed for a nap and decided it was time to quiz me with some of the chapter questions in the back of the book.

"How much of the Earth was made of water?" she asked.

"60… no, 70%!" I corrected myself. I remembered that, since it was such a big number.

"Good, and how many planets are in the Milky Way galaxy?"

"Uhh, 9," I responded.

"Can you name them?" she inquired.

"Mercury, Venus, Earth, Mars, Jupiter, Saturn, Uranus, Neptune, and Pluto!" I spouted, holding my arms up in triumph.

"Excellent!" My mom continued to quiz me, and while a lot of the questions I didn't know, like just how many people were on the earth at its highest peak (12 billion!), or what was the Earth's deepest point (the Mariana Trench- 36,070 feet below sea level), I knew way more than I thought I would. I guess studying pays off! She suggested I use the questions at the end of the chapters to make my own flash cards. I wrote the questions on one side of an index card and then wrote the answers to the questions on the backside of the card. That really helped, and by the time the weekend was over, I felt ready for my big test. I was still a little nervous… okay, a LOT nervous. But I felt confident that I could do my best and maybe pull off that A that would let me continue on to 7th grade.

As I curled up in bed that night, I could hardly sleep. I was so nervous. I'd heard that a good night's sleep is essential to doing your best work. So, forcing myself to take a deep breath, I rolled over and waited for sleep to come.

CHAPTER 10:
THE MOMENT OF TRUTH

I woke up to my alarm blaring and rolled over to hit the off button. Sitting up in bed, I immediately felt nauseous with a nervous energy. This was the day. The day of the big History test. This day was going to decide my entire life. Whether I was going to continue on to the seventh grade or be left behind for eternity. Whether my friends would still be in class with me or move on without me and replace me with new friends. And worst of all, whether I was going to be stuck repeating this History class next year too...

I took a deep breath, trying not to think about it. In order to distract myself, I set about getting ready for the day. Sniffing a T-shirt from a pile on the floor (it didn't smell too bad), I pulled it over my head and tucked it into my jeans. I brushed my teeth and my hair, slapped on some deodorant, and sprayed a little Galaxy body spray (you know, just in case the t-shirt was grosser than I thought). Then, grabbing my backpack, I headed downstairs.

My mom set a plate of waffles and bacon before me—my favorites! I doused them both in imitation maple syrup and watched my sister as she attempted to feed herself, managing to get it just about everywhere except her mouth.

"So, do you feel ready for your test today?" My mom asked as she sat at the table and tried to help my sister navigate at least some of her breakfast into her mouth.

"Kind of... I'm really nervous," I answered, fidgeting in my seat.

"You're going to do great, honey," my mom replied. "I know how hard you've tried, and I'm so proud of you! Just do your best, and we will take the outcome however it goes."

I nodded. "Thanks, mom."

As I was finishing my breakfast, I could hear the hoverbus coming down the street. I shoved the last bite of bacon in my mouth, swung my backpack over my shoulder, and headed out the door.

"Bye, sweetie, good luck!" my mom called behind me.

I waved goodbye and stepped onto the bus, taking my usual seat between Hero and Toejam.

"Hey man," Toe greeted me. "Feel ready for the test?"

"More or less..." I replied with a weak grin.

"No, you're supposed to say that you're more than ready, and you're going to do great," Hero replied. "That's called a self-fulfilling prophecy—if you believe you're going to do well, you will, and if you believe you'll do bad, you will!"

"Oh. Well, then yeah, I'm super ready. I studied all weekend," I replied, trying to project an air of confidence into my voice.

"That's the spirit! You got this!" Hero replied.

All throughout the morning, I could hardly sit still in my lectures. I wasn't paying attention at all. I was only fidgeting in my seat, sneaking peeks at my flashcards, and trying not to panic about the test that had my whole life on the line. Despite my nerves, the day seemed to fly by, and before I knew it, it was lunch time. I went through the line, got my food, and sat down at a table with Toe and Hero, a pit weighing heavy in the bottom of my stomach.

"Hey Dweeb," an all-too-familiar voice called from behind me, and I turned to see Chris standing over me. "I heard you're going to fail the sixth grade? How dumb can you be?" he laughed his cruel, hearty laugh at me.

"I mean, you only have a, what, 10% chance of passing?" Melvin chimed in, peering out from behind his beefy companion. "I doubt anyone will even remember you when the rest of us move on to seventh grade. We'll all be going upstairs to the upper classrooms, and you'll still be stuck down here, with the babies. I doubt we'll ever see you again. Heh heh, make sure you bring your lunch money tomorrow, Dweeb. I'm gonna want to cherish your last few days at school with us." Melvin laughed shrilly as he turned and walked away, Chris hot on his tail.

"Don't worry about them, Dwayne," Toe gave me a nudge. "They're just trying to get in your head. You're going to do fine."

"Fine isn't good enough; I have to get an A," I replied quietly.

"And you will!" Hero answered. "Everything's going to be okay! And next year, when we're all together, we'll make sure to do more studying together so none of us will fall behind again, okay?"

"Thanks, guys," I nodded, and tried to take a bite of my lunch. It was like chewing sawdust, so I just sat there and stabbed it with my plastic knife. As though in the blink of an eye, the bell rang, and it was time for class. I felt like I was walking to my grave as I stepped into that classroom and plopped down in my seat.

Heart racing, I waited in near panic for Mr. Hammond to enter the room. Would the test be multiple choice or short answer? How many questions? How hard would it be? These questions raced frantically around my mind, and by the time the door finally opened, I thought I might actually explode. Mr. H strolled into the room, giving his standard "good afternoon, class," greeting. "Today you are going to take your final exam. Please put everything away, keeping only 2 pencils on your desk. Write as neatly as possible and good luck." Then, he began to pass papers down the rows of seats.

When the test landed on my desk, I wrote my name at the top of it, before looking down at the rest of the paper, which read: History Essay Final.

There was only one question on the sheet: What was the most interesting thing you learned in class this year?

I felt my mind go blank as I heard the scratching of pencils on paper around me. I needed a topic. I needed it now. I needed to brainstorm. Jotting down the main idea of each chapter of the book, I stopped immediately when I came to the chapter I had liked the most in my history textbook: NASA. I'd spent the most time browsing that chapter and learning all about NASA's history. I could definitely write an essay on that. I took a deep breath as I picked up my pencil.

Okay. Here we go. First, an outline, which I decided to scribble on the side of the paper.

DWAYNE'S OUTLINE

I. Introduction

    A. Many people are familiar with space, but not a lot of people are familiar with how humans got started in exploring space.

    B. NASA was humanity's first leap into space exploration.

    C. NASA was important to send humans to the Aethur.

II. Body Paragraph 1

    A. Early space exploration
    B. Putting a man in orbit, sending a man to the moon, etc...

III. Body Paragraph 2

    A. Mars
    B. Mars Rover, Mission to Mars, Mars space station...

IV. Body Paragraph 3

    A. Modern History
    B. The Aethura Project, Aethur, etc...

V. Conclusion

    A. From the moon, to Mars, to the Aethur...
    B. NASA was vital to humanity's first exploration of space.
    C. NASA's small beginnings paved the way for humankind's migration to outer space.

With my outline complete and sitting before me, I took a deep breath, tried to focus, and then began to write.

DWAYNE'S ESSAY

Space exploration is something that most Aethurians are very familiar with, especially when it comes to the connection between outer space and our old planet, the Earth. But not many people think about the origin of space exploration, and where it all began. From early attempts to go to the moon, to Mars, to every other planet in the solar system, NASA was exponential in providing the foundation to send humans to the Aethur.

The National Aeronautics and Space Administration, or NASA, founded in 1958 by American President Dwight D. Eisenhower, marked the beginning of humankind's first real leap into space exploration. In 1957, the Soviets launched the very first satellite, Sputnik 1, into space. America launched its first satellite four months later. After NASA was established, they began to work on finding ways to send men into space. In 1961, Russians sent a man to orbit the Earth for about 108 minutes. Then, America managed the feat in 1962. It became a race for NASA to beat all other countries in the field of space exploration. After a few failed attempts, finally, in 1969, American Neil Armstrong was the first man to walk on the moon, where he said he took "one small step for man, one giant leap for mankind."

In the 1970s, the first space station was created, where astronauts could live in space in Earth's orbit long-term. The International Space Station was created for all space competitors to work together. The space station was continuously occupied from the year 2000 to when humans moved to the Aethur. It was serviced by visitors from more than 17 different countries, and was a stopping point for all who were working together on a quest to find a more viable planet for the human population.

In the year 2003, The Mars Rover "Opportunity" was deposited on Mars. After only 15 years on the planet, the Rover died, but the mission was not unsuccessful, for while there, it located water on the planet's surface. NASA was encouraged by the discovery of water and developed a plan to send men to Mars by the year 2030. Because of budget cuts and technical issues, this plan was not carried out until almost 2040, when NASA was able to send a small crew to the planet to deposit the initial materials to erect a crude construction to house future teams of explorers. They were unsure if life would be sustainable on Mars due to the huge dust storms that occur on the planet's surface, and the lack of oxygen. Ten years later, the first Martian space station was complete, which sparked NASA's explorations into deeper space. For the next few hundred years, NASA worked to discover and explore all of the planets in the solar system.

The need to branch out beyond the Earth's solar system led to The Aethura Project, which was developed in the year 2626 when it was evident that the human population had become far too much for the Earth to handle. The project searched for other galaxies which might contain a suitable planet to call home. Eventually, they discovered the Aethur in 2765, which led humanity to abandon the Earth for a whole new planet. Though the crucial need to find a suitable planet was met and humanity saved from destruction, Space exploration has continued to evolve. No longer used as an urgent necessity, space exploration has now become an affordable form of recreation for adventurous vacationers every year.

NASA was the beginning of humanity's move into space and was vital in creating the planet we know today. From the earliest attempts to go to the moon, then to Mars, and every other planet in the solar system and beyond, NASA's small beginnings paved the way for humankind's migration to outer space and a whole new way of life.

When I finished writing, I put my pencil down, and began to look over my work. I'd done a pretty good job, and I felt proud of my essay. I glanced at the time and found I even had about five minutes left before the bell, so I used the time to skim through and make sure I didn't have any spelling mistakes.

Then, the bell rang, and Mr. Hammond called, "Okay, pencils down. Turn in your exams. I will have them graded and given back to you tomorrow."

I followed my row out the door and placed my essay on the corner of Mr. H's desk with everyone else's. The minute I stepped out the door, I felt a sense of relief, and I was finally able to meet Hero and Toe with a big grin on my face. "I think that was an A essay."

"Dude, that's great!" Hero cheered.

"Awesome! We've gotta celebrate!" Toe grinned back.

"We've still got another class, we can't skip," I laughed, but Toejam began to dig in his backpack, removing three packages of chocolate candy.

"I knew you'd do well," he passed me a package, and we each quickly devoured the sweets, before heading into our last class together. I felt light as a feather with that big test out of the way, and I was practically walking on air as I stepped off of the hoverbus towards my house.

The next day at school dragged on excruciatingly slow. I was so nervous to find out what I got on my History exam. Would I be moving on to 7th grade or not? English class was pretty entertaining though. Mrs. Walker loved our essays! I guess the League of Lame Superheroes isn't so lame after all, because we all got A's. We also all got picked to read our essays in front of the class as examples on how to do the assignment correctly. The look on the Brian's' face was priceless when Mrs. Walker told him that his needed a lot of improvement and he had to rewrite it. She even suggested that he ask me for help if he couldn't figure it out. It was hilarious. He was gritting his big buck teeth so hard I thought he might draw blood, and I'm sure I literally saw steam leak out of his ears, he was so mad.

After what seemed like an eternity of waiting for every second of the day to creep by, the moment of truth had finally come. Entering history class and taking my seat, I couldn't seem to make my legs stop bouncing from the overflow of nervous energy.

Mr. H leisurely strolled into the room like he didn't have a care in the world. Meanwhile, I could feel the sweat trickle down the back of my neck, and I was sure I might vomit at any second. Finally, mercy prevailed, and he started handing back our tests. He placed mine face down on my desk and gave a maniacal little chuckle.

With a deep breath and a shaky hand, I flipped it over and gasped.

There, proudly displayed at the top of my test in Mr. H's darkest pen, was a great big F. I could hear the sound of the great inhales of air being sucked into the lungs of my friends. My lungs, they were empty, they weren't working, they were refusing to cooperate. I couldn't breathe. I just sat there, wide-eyed, confused, and utterly...

"Oh, I forgot something," Mr. H announced. Then he leaned over with the same thick black pen and ran a slash mark, angling from the top of the F to the bottom, turning the formidable letter from a nightmare to a fairytale as it became an A right before my eyes. "I was just having a little fun," he chuckled. "Great job. Incredible improvement, Dwayne." Then he proceeded to scratch out a plus sign. An A+, I got an A+. I was so excited that I leapt from my seat and hugged him right there in front of the whole history class. He just awkwardly slapped me on the back a few times. Then Toe, Hero and I were hi-fiving and fist bumping and whooping at the top of our lungs. So, The League of Lame Superheroes lives to fight again. Watch out seventh grade, here we come.

Made in the USA
Las Vegas, NV
16 September 2024